JOSÉ

(JOS)

A BILINGUAL
LIPOGRAMMATIC
TALE

GREGORIO C. PEDROZA, Ph.D.

Firekeeper Press, Apalachin, NY 13732

ISBN: 978-1-7370770-0-8

LOVINGLY DEDICATED

to

GRANDCHILDREN
NICHOLAS
CHELSEY
MARILIA
VICTORIA
SAMANTHA
DIAMOND MARIE
JOSHUA
DAVID
JOHN
EMERALD ANN

GREAT-GRANDCHILDREN
JULIAN
CATARINA
JOSEPH
JOHN
BILLY

CAVEAT

TO MY LOVING, LARGE EXTENDED FAMILY

I wrote this collection of stories to explore a new constrained method of writing, and more so, to illuminate our culture and the environment I experienced in my formative years. This is not an autobiography although I have used stories from my life experience, some of which may perhaps be familiar to you. I have borrowed stories from our large Arcos and Pedroza families. I have taken literary license, changing names and attributing stories to different people; however, the stories are true as seen through a little boy's eyes. The stories are not directly transportable to your ancestral family tree.

My intention is to awaken in you and all readers an appreciation of your own stories as you recall them.

ACKNOWLEDGEMENTS

Without Lilly, my wife, and her patience, love, and encouragement, this book would not have been possible. I also feel blessed to have such a vibrant and supportive immediate and extended family. They have charged me as the "The Keeper of the Story" for the younger generation. My extended family was the crucible for my formative years and my immediate family is the heart of my existence.

I express my gratitude to Suzanne Geoghegan for her expertise in English and Spanish and her gentle yet persistent critique. Her Spanish grammar was invaluable. I humbly thank Vivian Muñoz-Halm for her feedback after reading and introducing the stories to her high school Spanish class. I also appreciate Andy Bonetti, Christine Fisher, and Frank and Barbara Schlee's dedication and commentaries as readers.

Above all, I am grateful to Karen Bernardo who embraced this project and brought it to fruition. Karen brought everything together, adding her visual flair and organizational ability to produce this book, with which I am well pleased.

From the bottom of my heart—Mil Gracias.

TABLE OF CONTENTS

INTRODUCTION
THE LIPOGRAMMATIC STYLE AND THE BASIS OF THIS STORY

The *Merriam Webster Dictionary* defines a lipogram as a method of constrained writing—a sort of word game. The writing is composed of passages that intentionally omit a certain letter. The example given is the Greek work, the *Odyssey* by Tryphiodorus, in which he did not use the letter Alpha in the first book, Beta in the second book and so on.

This style does not make a work easier to write; in fact, it makes it a great deal more challenging. In this collection of vignettes, I've added an extra challenge by making the book bilingual. English and Spanish blend to enrich the reader's knowledge and pleasure.

STORY BASIS

These vignettes are based on my experiences growing up in a *barrio*. This is not precisely an autobiographical work. I call it nonfiction fiction. The events are true, but they have been described through the prism of a child's eye, and all the names have been changed. To a child the *barrio* seemed an ideal place to live. It was safe and secure; even though we were deemed poor and disadvantaged, I did not lack for the basics. Plus I had boundless love from family and community.

The stories cover the era from the mid-1940s to the mid-1950s. In the 40s the men were returning from war. On my father's side I had five uncles and my father in the service. On my mother's side I had five uncles serve. They served in Africa, Europe and throughout the Pacific and they all came home honorably. My understanding is that as an ethnic group Hispanics, percentage-wise, earned the most Congressional Medals of Honor of any other group. The Hispanic Medal of Honor Society states that 32 Hispanics earned the Medal in WWII and Korea. They fought for freedom and returned to segregation in jobs, housing and civil rights. I remember hearing about the fight to allow a hero who died in battle to be buried in the town's "Anglo" cemetery. Our men became plumbers, electricians, mechanics and activists.

The 50s brought more war, more uncles serving, more vets returning. Mass deportations were endured during the Wetback Program. The greatest change was brought about by the ruling of Brown vs. Board of Education in 1954, which began to end segregation in schools. In our small town, there were five schools. There was a two-room school on the outskirts of town for the Black community. The public elementary school for "Mexican" Spanish-speaking students was on the west side of town. The elementary school for Catholic Spanish-speaking students was north of the railroad tracks. The elementary school for Catholic English-speaking students was on the south side, while the elementary school for non-Catholic English-speaking students was near the high school. The high school was not segregated. But the elementary schools took many years to consolidate.

Every town in Texas had at least one *barrio*. This was the area where most Hispanics lived and, with no decision-making representation, these were the areas that were the last to receive services and utilities. In retrospect, it seems to me the *barrios* were seen as a convenient place to consolidate cheap labor. I choose to write these vignettes to depict life as I experienced it in spite of the turmoil in the outside world and the turmoil my parents and *barrio* had to endure. I was not ignorant of this turmoil but I chose to dwell on the positive.

In the late 40s we moved to the edge of the *barrio* closer to town and away from the flood zone. I was then blessed with two more beautiful sisters. My extended family is very large. My mother was number thirteen in a family of twenty-four, which includes two foster children. My father was number three in a family of eighteen children.

My grandmothers were strong, loving mothers who never learned to speak English. My mother and father each went as far as the sixth grade before they were needed at home. Out of this large clan of aunts, uncles and an over-abundance of cousins, I was the first one to go to college. My education continued and I attained a Doctor's Degree in Organic Chemistry. As the vanguard, I can look back and take pride at the many teachers, nurses, medical doctors, lawyers, college graduates and an ambassador I can count as family. The family has gone from the confines of the *barrio* to the halls of Harvard University in two generations.

I hope this work will inspire my readers to recall the forces that formed their lives and the sacrifices made by their ancestors.

Which way should I face
With my innocent child's gaze
To find the source—to find the place
Where the seeds of hope were planted
A long time ago

MI BARRIO

A *barrio* is a neighborhood
I want this understood
Not a slum, not a ghetto
It's my home
Mi barrio

In the morning of my life
A long time ago
With my eyes wide open
Heart unbroken
I was born
In the *barrio*

My spirit was unfettered
With dreams that it was fed
I looked not at the negative
Did not dwell on what was not
I was taught to speak the positive
And give thanks for what I've got

Some say *mi barrio*
Was not a good place to live
No work, no money
No food in our cupboards
For our children to give
Some say *mi barrio* lacked for much
Others talk of so and so
Or mention such and such
Some see the lack of water,

Sewer system, paved streets,
No doors and the lack of solid floors
In the morning of my life
A long time ago
With my eyes wide open
Heart unbroken
I was growing up
In *mi barrio*

La Marrana, El Caballo, El Comino
Los Pelones, Juan Tonto y Yo
I know where to go
I can find these friends
En mi barrio.

When it rained it would pour
Bringing water snakes and frogs
Right through our front door
So off to high ground we would go—
La Marrana, El Caballo, El Comino,
Los Pelones, Juan Tonto y Yo

In the morning of my life
A long time ago
With our eyes wide open
Spirits unbroken
We were proud to live
In *mi barrio.*

Which way should I face
With my innocent child's gaze

To find the source—to find the place
Where the seeds of hope were planted
A long time ago
But with eyes wide open
Heart unbroken
To my *mamá* and *papá's* praying
En el barrio

Two-room nest
Papá did his best
Hardwood floor
Mamá's chore
No heat, no plumbing
Outhouse humming
Flies buzzing through
A new moon rising
On a droopy door

Dream your dreams
Suppress your screams
Yo se que con ganas
Todo se puedo
En el Barrio de las Ranas

Take what you can
Love of family—love of friend
Sharing and caring
Abrazos y regazos
Dancing and romancing
Mouth-watering aromas of
Tortillas con frijoles

And *menudo con pozoles*
In the twilight of my life
With little life to go
And my eyes wide open
Heart unbroken
I am proud to be a product of
Mi barrio.

CHAPTER I
JOSÉ'S FISHING TRIP
(NO A STORY)

José lived in the little white house on the edge of *el pueblito*, the little town. His mother lived there. His sister Consuelo lived there. His pop lived there too. The house's rooms were the big living room plus the not-so-big kitchen where his mother cooked delicious food, so they spent more time in the kitchen. There were two bedrooms—one for the two grown-ups, one for the children. José's best friend, Pepino, his *perrito* or little dog, lived outside with his other best friend, Beto the burro.

Mother cooked, Consuelo helped, Pop provided for everyone. He worked tending their field where he grew most of their food. Next door lived Tío Simón, José's uncle, with his wife Dolores. José liked to work with his Pop, but he loved to fish with Tío Simón.

One evening José wiped down his fishing pole. He unrolled the line, then inspected the hook. With the line looking sturdy, the hook with the cork further up the line tied securely, José shivered with excitement. The next morning José went hurriedly to get his stringed fishing pole. Excitedly he scurried to meet Tío Simón. Before going to meet Tío Simón, he confidently promised his mom fresh fish for dinner. José's mom nodded, smiling, while José left the house.

Seeing José's excitement, Tío Simón grinned. "José, did you finish your chores?" Tío Simón wondered.

"Yes!" shouted José. He knew how Tío Simón loved to joke.

Tío Simón strolled with José to the creek which flowed by the edge of the fields. Tío Simón fished the creek very often. He knew where the deep *pozos,* holes, were—the deep *pozos* where the big fish lived. Tío Simón chuckled seeing José jumping, skipping the entire trip to the creek. Tío Simón knew fishing required sitting quietly, no noise, looking for the cork to bob. When the cork bobbed, this told him the fish were biting the lure, possibly getting hooked. José would need to experience this for himself to become skillful like Tío Simón.

José got to the creek first. Quickly unrolling his line, he put two worms on the hook before tossing it into the creek. Tío Simón showed him how to move the line slowly without jerking it or knocking the worms off. José wished the fish would bite quickly so he could hook them. He could see the little fish nibbling his worms. The big silvery fish just looked, swimming slowly, checking out the juicy worms.

José fidgeted while he urged the big fish to come dine on the delicious plump worms. "Come on, big fish. Come see how good you will feel dining on the nice worms," whispered José.

The fish just circled slowly, inspecting the worms, possibly looking for the hook. They were wise big fish for they knew not to rush. They knew to look for hooks, to look for tricks, but José's two worms hid the hook well. The worms wiggled. The little fish surrounded the worms nibbling. The big fish seeing the little fish dining, shot quickly, fins whirling, bubbles spewing. The little fish scurried. The big fish gulped the two worms with the entire pointy hook.

José felt the fish hit the hook. The cork jiggled while bobbing. The cork went down quickly. José jumped, lifted the pole, jerking the line. Tío Simón told him to do this in order to set the hook.

Seeing José jerk the line, Tío Simón jumped up to help. José looked white with excitement but he did not let go of the pole. The hooked fish did not like the hook in his mouth. The fish tried to spit it out but José kept the line tight. The fish jerked, jumped, flopped but José held on to the pole while digging his feet into the dirt in order not to be pulled into the creek by the huge fish.

José shouted with joy when Tío Simón with his tremendous strength helped him tug on the line, pulling the fish to shore. Tío Simón's smile just got wider when he lifted José off the ground. José quickly pounced on the flopping fish. He could not control his excitement. He shouted. He whistled. Monkey-like, he bounced up screeching, tumbled down screeching. José just went wild. He hooked the biggest fish of his young life. It did not look silvery. It looked negro, old, with big whiskers. José's mom would be proud of him. Tío Simón sure looked proud, struggling to put the big fish on José's string.

Tío Simón fished no more with José. They went home full of joy, showing off their huge ebony fish to the cheering neighbors. Tío Simón told everyone how José hooked the ferocious fish by himself.

José's mom could not believe the size of the fish. They would need to cut it up just to fit it into the pot. She would fry some of it in oil. She would use the rest in thin broths or in her delicious spicy thick fish stew. Very proud of José, his mom cooked some of the big fish for dinner. She invited the neighbors to join them. The whole neighborhood enjoyed José's fish. José just blushed when they lifted him up on their shoulders shouting, "¡José! ¡José! ¡José!"

José loved spending time with friends and family, the people he loved most in the world.

CHAPTER II
JOSÉ'S FAMILIA Y AMIGOS
(NO B STORY)

Alicia was José's *mamá* and everyone called her Licha. She was tall, long-haired, and always wore a pleasant smile. She worked hard keeping the house in order, cooking delicious meals, tending to José and Consuelo and helping their *papá* take care of the garden and animals. Licha was seen as the happy light in the family.

Papá's name was Manuel and everyone called him Manolo. Well, everyone except Licha. Licha called him Meme. Manolo worked the land all day. He had a huge garden where he grew food for the family and plenty of produce to sell in the market in town. His garden was on a good piece of land and not too far from the *arroyo*, the creek. Even in the dry season, the land kept some moisture.

Manolo raised *tomates*; *lechuga* or lettuce; *frijoles* or legumes; *ajo*, garlic; *pepinos*, cukes; *chile dulce*, sweet peppers; *chile jalapeño*, hot chiles; *sandía,* watermelon; *melón,* cantaloupe; and other fruits and veggies that sold well in the market. He also had a small orchard. José loved the *nueces,* pecans, the most for they kept very well through the winter. The *duraznos,* peaches, *uvas,* grapes and *peras,* pears were juicy and delicious, and that is why most of them were sold in the market.

Consuelo was younger than José and she spent most of her time following Mamá or playing with her *muñecas,* dolls. She loved the little *muñequita* Mamá had made out of an old sock. It had yarn for hair, a pretty dress, huge honey-colored eyes and a sunny smile. Consuelo called her

Chachita. She would play with Chachita for hours. When Papá made a *cuna* or cradle for Chachita, Consuelo would lay Chachita down to change her, and for her naps.

Tío Simón lived on one side of José's house, and Grandpa and Grandma lived on the other. José was really lucky, for Tío Simón loved to fish and Grandpa loved to talk. José could spend hours listening to the stories from Mexico. He especially liked to listen to stories of Pancho Villa and the Revolution while eating Grandma's honey-filled *sopapillas*. Grandma would just smile seeing Grandpa with that faraway look in his eyes, and José paying rapt attention with honey dripping down his chin.

Not too far away lived his friends Ignacio—everyone called him Nacho—and Armando, known as Mando. José, Nacho and Mando liked to go on adventures in the mesquite and oak-filled woods, or go exploring along the edge of the *arroyo* looking for *ranas* or frogs, *peces* or fish, *camarones* or crawfish, and even *serpientes*, snakes. They would spend all afternoon just watching and wondering and imagining. José especially liked to show Nacho and Mando the exact spot where he had caught the huge fish.

José loved spending time with friends and family, the people he loved most in the world.

CHAPTER III
JOSÉ Y MANDO
(NO C STORY)

One day Mando asked José's *mamá* if José was home. He wanted to play. She said, "No, José is helping his father water the garden." Mando went to the garden and seeing that José and his father, Manolo, were working hard and laughing hard, he joined in the fun.

With Mando's help, they finished watering early and José had time to play before supper. José and Mando looked at one another, winked and nodded. For a few days they had been talking about an interesting idea. They were now ready to start.

José and Mando had wondered how many types of *ojas* or leaves there were just around the house. Their goal was to start by finding five good leaves and identifying them before supper. They first went to the house and asked Mamá for wax paper. She was puzzled as to why they wanted wax paper, but when they explained that they wanted to press the leaves in order to save them, she gave them a whole roll.

José borrowed the *tijeras* or shears from Abuelita, the name they gave Grandma. She did not give them the pointy, sharp ones she used for sewing, but instead she gave them little ones with rounded ends. They were safer for running around in the woods. Mando got a paper bag from his *mamá* and they headed toward the trees.

The first *oja* they gathered was from the old mesquite tree near Beto the burro's stall. The *ojas* of the mesquite tree were small and shaped like fat needles. José liked them for in the *otoño* or fall, he did not have to rake them. The *ojas* were so small, they just pulverized.

Mando took a stem of mesquite leaves and pressed them in a little envelope he had made from the wax paper. Mando said, *"¡Una oja!"* "One leaf!" It was a very little *oja* but it was their first.

"Oh, so you want a big *oja,*" said José. "I will show you the biggest *oja* we have." He led Mando to the *árbol de higos,* the fig tree.

"¡Híjole!" shouted Mando. "I'll have to make a giant envelope to fit a leaf from the *higo* tree."

José just smiled as he snapped off a big, green leaf from the *higo* tree. A white milky sap oozed from the severed stem of the leaf. The leaf had a beautiful shape and what looked like thin short white hairs all over it. It was not as smooth as it looked from afar.

“*¡Dos ojas!*” yelled Mando as he put the leaf in the huge envelope, making sure he did not bend or break it. The envelope barely fit in the bag.

They walked deeper into the woods on the way to the *arroyo.* Mando wanted to make sure they got a leaf from the giant *roble,* oak, where they loved to play on sunny afternoons. The *roble* looked one hundred years old. José’s Abuelito, Grandfather, told stories about how the mighty *roble* would not bend to the wind; its stubbornness was sometimes the reason why the *roble* would break or be uprooted. The *roble* was always green. It dropped its leaves all the time as new ones grew in. Mando found a shiny brown leaf on the ground and José took a shiny green one from the tree.

"¡Tres ojas!" they both shouted as they put them in their bag.

As they walked, Mando and José talked about leaves. The *nopal* had leaves but they were big and fat and had sharp needles. They agreed that this time they would not get a leaf from the *nopal.* They also passed by the *maguey,* or agave, with its very large leaves with pointy sharp spikes all along the edge and at the tip. When they saw the *nogal,* though, José knew he wanted that leaf, for this was the tree that gave the sweet-tasting nuts he loved to eat. The leaf from the *nogal* or nut tree was long and shiny and had a smooth edge. No sharp needles or spikes here. They now had four leaves.

Mando liked to rest under the shade of the tree he named El Llorón, the weeping willow. The leaves of the weeping willow had different shades of green. In the *primavera*, spring, the leaves were a yellow green. Later in the summer they turned a darker green. The leaves were almost feathery as they hung sadly from the limbs and waved mournfully with the slightest breeze.

"Yes," said Mando, "this is my favorite tree."

José knew the weeping willow was not stubborn like the oak. They gathered the best stem of leaves they were able to find, put it in the envelope and smiled.

They had met their goal of five leaves before supper. When they got home they showed their leaf treasure to José's *mamá.* She smiled and said that after supper she would help them press the leaves into the wax paper with her hot iron. This way the leaves would keep their shapes and bright hues forever.

CHAPTER IV
JOSÉ Y NACHO
(NO D STORY)

José *y* Nacho were *amigos.* Even when working or eating or just walking, José *y* Nacho were having fun playing together. They usually met at the *arroyo.* They sat quietly, waiting to see what animal came to get water or something to eat.

There were no big animals, just little ones because it was almost noon. Most animals came very early or late in the evening, but José *y* Nacho were there late in the morning, when the sun was hot. So the boys sat very quietly.

Soon a *conejito,* a rabbit, came near the water, looking nervous but also looking thirsty. The *conejito* took one last hop before putting his nose near the water, satisfying his thirst. He then quickly took a big hop into the safety of the bushes. José *y* Nacho just sat there smiling, feeling lucky to have seen a *conejito.*

"The animals that live in the water are not easy to spot either," thought José. Crawling, they got closer to the water. Laying there quietly, barely breathing, José *y* Nacho soon saw a green *ranita,* a little frog. The *ranita* was very still in the water with only her eyes above the surface. She was looking at the boys, checking them out, making sure they were no threat to her.

After a while the *ranita* swam out of the water, still cautious but with no fear of José *y* Nacho. The *ranita* actually came right up to their faces. Maybe she thought the freckles on Nacho's nose were small bugs to eat. Nacho, nose twitching, gave out a big sneeze, blowing the little *ranita* back into the water. José *y* Nacho almost burst themselves laughing.

Then they both got quiet again. Both listening, slowly turning, they saw a big cottonmouth snake sneaking up on the poor little *ranita.* Jumping, shouting, scrambling, they threw rocks at the snake. The snake shot into the tall grass in the shallows. The *ranita* safely swam away to the other shore of the little *arroyo.* She got out of the water, hopping far away from the creek, far away from the snake. José *y* Nacho were glad they were quick to scare the snake away, saving the *ranita* from becoming the snake's snack.

José *y* Nacho were happy to see many little minnows swimming with no big fish to eat them. This time they were not able to scare up any *camarones* or crawfish. José *y* Nacho were very partial to *camarones con huevos,* crawfish with eggs, the way José's *mamá* knew how to prepare them.

They soon got hungry so they ran home. They knew José's *mamá* was fixing a great lunch of tacos with *frijoles con huevos.* A big glass of *leche,* milk, was waiting for them as they came in the *cocina* or kitchen. The special mouth-watering aroma of *tacos* was all through the *cocina.* Mamá Licha, smiling, put a big plate of *tacos* in front of the boys. Looking at each other, José y Nacho ate with gusto. Maybe next time *camarones,* but not this time. This time their meal after their trip to the *arroyo* was *tacos* with *frijoles con huevos.* José was so very lucky to have such a loving mother as his *mamá*, Licha.

That amor of Licha y Manolo shot sparks all around to also show amor to all.

CHAPTER V
LICHA Y MANOLO
(NO E STORY)

First and always at all hours of day or night, Licha y Manolo would think of *familia*—family. *Familia* was all-important to Licha *y* Manolo. Licha's instincts would prod thoughts of that growing *niño,* boy, who had a curious mind and a happy disposition. Licha also thought of that charming *muchachita,* small girl, who too soon would grow into a vivacious young lady. In addition, Manolo thought of Grandpa and Grandma. Grandpa and Grandma, old but not sick, *gracias a Dios.* Licha *y* Manolo had faith that God and hard work would always triumph.

Manolo's crop-growing plot, his *milpa*, with its cool moist soil, would sustain *la familia* with nourishing, scrumptious food. It took much hard work, but Manolo did not mind working hard. Working for *la familia* was his mission and honor. Manolo would work all day from dawn to dusk and did not complain. Manolo's *amor* for *la familia* was known to all, and all around him would clap with admiration.

Licha's ability to cook and constantly show *la familia* how to laugh was this *mamá's* gift. Licha was a happy soul and happily was how Licha sang for all. Licha's songs told of *amor* that Licha *y* Manolo had. That *amor* of Licha *y* Manolo shot sparks all around to also show *amor* to all. Licha, though living in spartan surroundings, was totally happy with Manolo, *los niños, y la familia.*

But Licha *y* Manolo still would think and at night worry about *la familia. La familia* was growing. Licha *y* Manolo, proud of how *la familia* was doing and growing, still would always pray for all at night.

Diosito, look at our familia with compassion.
Show us how to follow your plan,
How to always look for your ways,
Doing your will and not ours.
May our faith and trust in you grow daily.
Gracias, Diosito, for your gift of our familia.

Licha y Manolo would pray with passion, as so many moms and dads do.

CHAPTER VI
CONSUELO
(NO F STORY)

Consuelo looked like a little angel. She had very dark black eyes with long curly lashes. Her little mouth just gleamed when she smiled and one could see her little pearly white baby teeth. Her hair was like her *mamá's,* jet black. It had a natural wave. Mamá would wind her curls and they would cascade down her back below her shoulders. Consuelo had a good disposition and very seldom cried. As long as she could hear her *mamá* singing, she knew all was right with the world.

Mamá Licha had used a clean old sock to make Consuelo a doll. Consuelo could not say *muchachita,* girl, so she called the girl Chachita. Chachita's body, the sock, was packed with clean rags but not too tight. It was just right when cuddled. With black yarn Mamá had made Chachita's long hair. It looked a little like Consuelo's hair. She also had large brown button eyes with long painted lashes and a cute little smile just like Consuelo's. Mamá had also made Chachita a pretty dress with bright birds. Consuelo imagined she could hear the birds sing.

Abuelita Antonia, her grandma, had also made Consuelo a doll. She made it with cornhusks just like the one her *mamá* made when she was a little girl in Mexico. The doll was not a girl doll. It was a *muñequito*, a boy doll. Consuelo could not say *muñequito* either. So she called the doll Quito. Quito was just as tall as Chachita except he had arms and legs. His eyes were painted, as were his mouth and nose. Quito had a little *sombrero de charro*, a Mexican cowboy hat, which made him look very happy. With his arms out, his legs bent a little and his head thrown back, he looked like he was singing a love song or maybe he wanted to dance.

Consuelo would play with Chachita and Quito every day. Papá had made her a wooden *cuna,* or crib, and a wooden *caballito*—little horse. While Consuelo and Chachita made mud *tortillas* or played setting a table with her toy dishes, Quito would ride his horse. Consuelo loved to have Chachita and Quito dance just like her *mamá* and *papá* danced. It made Consuelo happy to see Mamá and Papá dance, so she would make Chachita and Quito dance too.

No matter how tired Papá was at the day's end, he always was ready to dance with Licha, his singing happy queen.

When it came time to take a nap, Quito would lay in the toy *cuna* while Consuelo and Chachita would lay beside it. Mamá would look down and count three little angels sound asleep. Very quietly she would continue to hum an old lullaby just like the one her mother hummed when she was a little baby.

Consuelo, Chachita and Quito would breathe gently and even smile in their sleep, knowing they were much loved.

Abuelito, with a teary look in his tired eyes, would stare into space as if to make sure he remembered every detail, and continue with his story.

CHAPTER VII
ABUELITO
(NO G STORY)

"I was born in Mexico in a little *aldea,* a little town, up in the mountains in the state of Jalisco. The mountains had abundant silver and an abundance of poor *peones,* laborers, who worked the mines. The riches left with the people who owned the mines and only a little stayed so the people would not starve."

When Abuelito started his story, José instantly was mesmerized. The world did not exist around him, for he was lost in Abuelito's world. Abuelito, with a teary look in his tired eyes, would stare into space as if to make sure he remembered every detail, and continue with his story. Abuelito and José, joined in spirit, would travel back to the yesterdays of Abuelito's childhood.

Abuelito would continue, "I was named Doroteo just like my father and I had six brothers and sisters. I was the middle child but I am the only one left. My father was struck by a thunderbolt from the sky while he was with the mule and plow in a field. Yes, that day we lost him, *que en Dios descanse,* may he rest in peace, and we also lost the mule. We did not know what to do, for all seven of us were little. Mamá, her name was Panchita, took sick with a flu that was the cause of a lot of fevers, and we lost her too. *Pobrecita,* poor soul, she left us when she went to join Papá in Heaven."

Abuelito would sit very quietly. José would patiently wait, for he knew that after a short pause and a deep breath Abuelito would continue.

"*Mi'jo,* my son," Abuelito would say as he started anew, "the times were hard. Some of my brothers and sisters, the little ones, went to live with relatives. My older brothers and I were left to take care of ourselves. None of us were in school and none of us were really able to take care of all of us. I loved to participate in the choir in church. The priest said that I had a beautiful voice. The priest and the nun fixed a place for me where I could sleep, so I stayed there.

"In the daytime I would work in a *tiendita,* a little store. I would sweep the store, stock the produce and make the deliveries. The owner of the store fed me lunch and started to teach me my numbers. The nun helped me with my letters. By the time I was fourteen I knew simple arithmetic and how to read and write."

Abuelito paused and looked down at José with a wide smile. He was proud that he knew his letters.

Then Abuelito continued, "I remember the day I started my second job. Now I could work, not just for food, but for money as well. Because I knew how to read and write, and because the town recorder had left town, I was chosen to do his job. I would record who died, who was born, who left town, who moved into town and who married. Everyone was happy. The *alcalde,* the mayor, was happy because I paid attention to details, and I was happy because with one job I could earn my food and with the other I could save a little money. What's more, I still had my little *rinconcito,* my little corner, on the floor to sleep in at the church. My salary was paid by the Federal State. This is where the problem started."

Abuelito stopped to take a drink of water, shift his position, and rub his arthritic limbs. He continued. "It was around 1910 and the Revolutíon would soon reach every little *aldea,* every town, in Mexico. I prayed we were safe and would not be affected because we were up in the mountains away from the main politics of the country, but I learned differently. My heart was with Pancho Villa and the *revolutíonarios.* After all, Pancho's real name was Doroteo like mine and he was for the *peones.* He wanted to throw out the rich thieves in the capital who looked only to line their own pockets while the country starved. I did not want to do battle with anyone for I knew I could not shoot at anyone, but my heart was with Pancho and the cause. Unfortunately, my salary was paid by the Federal State, the same people Pancho wanted to throw out!

"One day the *Federales* came into town. They rode fast horses and the buttons on their uniforms reflected the sun. What scared me most were their weapons. They had rifles and pistols and they threatened everyone with them. They were like *cucarachas,* cockroaches. What they did not eat, they took with them and what they did not take with them, they spoiled.

"The *Federalistas* wanted to know if there were any revolutionarios in our town. They came to me as the keeper of the records and demanded I tell them if I knew anyone. I was scared. They told me that they would shoot anyone they found that supported Pancho. Now I was really scared!

"Fortunately they soon left and I relaxed. I went about my business with my jobs. One day the store owner told me that he had visited a town down the mountain. He heard that Pancho and his men would come into a town, find anyone that worked or sympathized with the *Federalistas* and shoot them. Now I was terrified."

Here Abuelito would pull out his red bandana which he used as a handkerchief, take off his sombrero and wipe his face and head.

"I did not know what to do," Abuelito would say. "If I stayed, one or the other war party or army squad would come into town and I would be sunk. So I decided to leave Mexico. It was hard to leave my friends, my benefactors, my brothers and sisters. I was sixteen when I started on foot with very little money and only the clothes I wore on my back. It took me a year to walk the six hundred kilometers to Texas—and one of these days I will tell you that story." Abuelito closed his eyes, put his head back, and in a little while he was sound asleep.

José just sat there very quietly in the cool shade of the live oak tree. He was still with Abuelito in Mexico. He wondered what he would have done or where he would be now if Abuelito had not been brave. Because Abuelito had been brave, he, José, was here today, safe with a *mamá* and a *papá* and *abuelitos* and a sister and friends to love. José soon was asleep also. Abuelito and José were one in spirit.

CHAPTER VIII
JOSÉ LEARNS TO SWIM
(NO H STORY)

El arroyo, stream, was José's playground. José loved to explore it, listen to it or just rest by it. José's *mamá* did not like for José to go alone. "I am scared for you to be alone because you do not swim. Deep water and non-swimming boys do not mix. Do not go near *el arroyo* until you learn to swim," Mamá would say.

José wanted badly to learn to swim so José went to see Tío Simón. Tío knew a lot about water and swimming. Tío always joked about *el río* Simón swam to get to Texas. Tío Simón said *el río* was deep and swift but Tío swam so fast not even *sus pantalones* got wet. It was an old joke but Tío Simón liked to tell it and swore it was true. Nobody believed Tío's story. Anyway Tío Simón was ready and willing to instruct José on all fine points of swimming.

On a warm sunny Saturday afternoon José and Tío Simón went to *el arroyo*. "First," Tío Simón said, "move your arms like a windmill."

José rotated one arm.

"No, move two arms," said Tío Simón.

José moved two arms. José's arms were moving so fast, José was getting dizzy.

"Slow down!" cried Tío Simón.

"But I want to swim fast," said José.

"First learn to swim slowly. Later you can practice and learn to swim fast," said Tío Simón.

José grinned.

Next Tío Simón told José to jump in, but only waist deep. "Now put your face in and blow bubbles," instructed Tío Simón. José tried but a nose full of water was not to José's liking. José sputtered and spewed. Soon José's entire face was under water and José was not afraid to blow bubbles.

José jumped as a little *ranita,* frog, bumped José's leg.

Tío Simón grinned and said, "You are not alone. Many of God's little creatures live *en el arroyo*."

"Well, tell God's little creatures I just want to play, and not to bite me," cried José.

José played for some time. Soon José felt comfortable. Lying in not-too-deep water and staying really still, José started to float. José turned over and floated face down.

"Yes!" cried Tío Simón, "You now can do a dead man's float."

Tío Simón and José swam all afternoon and by dinnertime, José knew all about swimming. "Now all you need is practice," said Tío Simón.

And so José practiced strokes in bed, kicking in Mamá's little tub, or keeping very still as if floating. Eventually after many Saturday afternoons and many lessons by Tío Simón, José learned to swim. Everyone was proud of José. Yes, everyone was proud but José's *mamá* still would not let José go swimming alone.

"It is never safe to go swimming alone," Mamá would say. José obeyed Mamá. It was a small favor to ask.

CHAPTER IX
MANDO Y NACHO
(NO I STORY)

Mando, Nacho and José loved to hunt for rocks. When José was busy at the garden, Mando and Nacho would go alone. Later they would share what they had found.

One day José was busy so Mando and Nacho went to hunt for rocks alone. They wanted to add to the large number of rocks they had at Nacho's house. They had heard that there had been a storm up north. Maybe the water would carry or uncover new rocks by the *arroyo*. So off they went. Nacho had a bag, Mando a short pole to use as a probe.

When they got to the *arroyo*, they saw that the water had cut a new channel. The old *arroyo* bed was exposed and a new bed had been formed. Mando and Nacho shouted gleefully as they ran to the newly-uncovered treasure trove. There were thousands of rocks to check out. Some were too large, others were just common gravel, but many were colorful and had odd shapes.

Mando had a method. Mando would walk around and use the pole to turn rocks around. Mando would search an area fast. He looked only for colored rocks. Yellow rocks, green rocks, red rocks, black rocks, any rock that had color, Mando would look at. He would take only the small ones that maybe changed colors as he got them wet or as they reflected the sun. Mando was happy to see so many newly-exposed rocks.

Nacho had another method. He sat down and would not move. He would then look all around at every rock, stone or pebble he could reach. Nacho looked for unusually-shaped rocks, rocks that when broken open may show the shape of creatures trapped thousands and thousands of years ago. He had a group of shelled creatures, curly creatures, feathery creatures and even bugs and leaves.

Soon Mando had a handful of stones of all colors. One pretty pebble was dark green. He had never found one so green before. Once he found one that changed color when wet. José's grandfather who knew about rocks called that rock an opal. They kept that pretty rock apart from all the others.

Nacho had found an oddly-shaped chunk of shale. He looked at the edge and saw layers, bands of colors. He knew that layered rock was a good place for trapped creatures to be.

Mando and Nacho walked home because the sun was hot. They went to show José's *abuelo,* grandfather, the rocks they had found. Abuelo Doroteo would study the rocks and tell them what they were.

Abuelo looked at Mando's dark green rock. He turned the rock, felt the rock, saw how the sun came through the rock. "Sorry, Mando, not a rock. You have found a small ball of glass that has been made smooth by the water," stated the *abuelo*.

Mando was not sad. He would call the rock "nature's marble." He also had a lot of marbles.

Next, the *abuelo* looked at Nacho's shale stone. The *abuelo's* small hammer gently rapped the edge of the rock. The rock cracked open. He held the two halves and looked at them closely.

"¡Aha!" shouted the *abuelo*. "Here we have the shells of some mono-valve mollusks. We would call the mollusk a *caracol*."

Nacho jumped for joy. He had others but not as perfect as the one he had just found.

Mando and Nacho showed the treasured rocks to José, then added them to those they shared. Mando and Nacho had had a good afternoon rock hunt and they went home very happy.

We traveled mostly by night. If we slept at night we would sleep between the railroad tracks. Someone told us that snakes would not cross the railroad tracks. This meant that one of us had to stay awake in case a train was coming.

CHAPTER X
ABUELITA'S STORY
(NO J STORY)

Abuelita Antonia was a short lady with sharp black eyes and a ready smile. Abuelito would say that he was *el macho*—the man—of the house, but everybody knew who was the boss. Abuelita had had a hard life so she always made sure that there was plenty of everything in case of an emergency. She would buy one-hundred pound sacks of rice and beans and flour. The rice and beans she cooked in many ways from soups to *enchiladas*, and the flour was for the *tortillas* she made fresh every day.

Abuelita and Abuelito had twenty-four children and Licha was one of the youngest. Licha was the only one that chose to stay in the barrio and take care of them. All the others had moved to other towns, states—even other countries. Of the twenty-four, only sixteen had reached adulthood and Abuelita loved them all. She was the perfect example of what unconditional love should look like.

As soon as Abuelita sat down, the grandchildren—Licha's two, and the other children in the *barrio*—would gather around her. They knew that Abuelita would tell them a story. They loved to hear of how Abuelita got to this country.

"Pues yo no conoci ni a mi papá ni a mi mamá." "I did not know either my mother or my father," said Abuelita with a sad look on her face. The children's eyes opened wide; they were amazed at the unimaginable revelation. Abuelita would continue, "I remember when I was a little girl in Mexico. I lived in a *choza*, a hovel, with my two

stepbrothers who were older than me. They told me that my *mamá* had passed away when I was a baby and that Papá had disappeared a few years after that. I do not know exactly when, because I am not sure what year or what month I was born."

The children's mouths dropped open. Imagine not knowing when your birthday is!

Abuelita would smile and catch up with her story. "One day, when I was maybe eight or nine years old, my brothers came to tell me that we were going to *El Norte.* I could not believe what they were saying. *El Norte* was a magical place where one could get everything one needed. There was work, work that paid enough to live on and even to save. To go to *El Norte* was a dream.

"We started packing. I packed my only other dress and a change of underwear. That is all I had. I looked around to see what else I could take with me, but we had nothing else. I remembered the *delantal*, apron, that they told me my *mamá* had made. It was worn from so much washing but the reds and yellows and blues of the thread that my *mamá* had used to embroider it were still bright. I packed the *delantal* in my bundle. My only other treasured possession was the cornhusk doll they told me my mother had made for me. I wrapped it in the spare dress in the bundle. I then took off my *huaraches,* sandals, and packed them. In Mexico I could go barefoot but once in *El Norte* I wanted to wear my *huaraches*.

"After walking several days we came to a big *río.* The Mexicanos call it *El Río Bravo* but the Gringos call it the Rio Grande. My brothers had no money to pay the *coyote*, the smuggler, to take us across in a boat so we had to find a place to swim across. The night was very dark, no moon, no stars. I was afraid. All we could hear was rushing water. We came to the spot where we were told the water was not too deep and prepared to go in.

"'Psst, psst,' we heard from the bushes. 'Don't go in. It is too swift.'

"It was a group of other people who also were trying to cross. They said that they had a long rope and that one of them was a strong swimmer. They tied the rope to his waist, he walked a distance upriver and dove in. By the time he made it across, the current had carried him down river across from us. With the rope tied at both sides of the river we started to cross. First we took off all our clothes down to our underwear. I was glad it was dark and no one could see me very well. My brothers tied our clothes bundles on their heads. Then we tied ourselves together with another rope. I was in the middle with a brother in front of me and one behind. For them the water was not deep but I, being short, sank up to my neck right away.

"We grabbed the long rope and started to cross. There must have been a storm upriver because we saw dead animals and tree limbs drift by. I went under a few times but my brothers kept the rope tight so I could keep my head above water. I wanted to scream but we were told to keep very quiet. We finally sputtered across. We lay on the grassy bank, panting and huffing. As soon as we got our breath, we scurried into the bushes. I started to cry because I had stepped on some thorns. My brothers put their hands over my mouth and told me not to cry. They said that *La Migra,* the immigration patrol, or *Los Rinches,* Texas Rangers, would catch us and send us right back. But anyway, now we were in *El Norte* and I needed to put my *huaraches* on.

"We had brought no water or food. All we knew was that to get to where there was work we had to go north. We followed the railroad tracks. During the day we kept the rising sun to our right and the setting sun to our left. Texas was a dry, scrub-brush, cactus filled land. Everything had thorns and there were many things that wanted to bite you. I was mostly afraid of rattlesnakes. We ate the few berries we could find and drank cactus water.

"We traveled mostly by night. If we slept at night we would sleep between the railroad tracks. Someone told us that snakes would not cross the railroad tracks. This meant that one of us had to stay awake in case a train was coming. If we slept during the day we would hide in the thorny bushes, and again one of us had to stay awake to alert us if they saw anyone coming. Some good people at ranches would let us drink from their wells where the cattle were drinking and some even gave us pieces of bread to eat.

"After walking about one hundred and fifty miles we came to a valley where they were building a dam to make a reservoir for irrigation. My brothers found work and we were assigned a tent to live in. I cooked and washed for my brothers. Soon I was making extra money washing for the other men. Each day I would make a mountain of *tortillas* and at noon I would sell bean *tacos* to the workers.

"I was almost twelve when a handsome seventeen-year-old young man walked into camp. He had no family and knew no one, so my brothers asked him to stay with us until he could find a place to live." Here Abuelita would sigh and with a big smile say, "And here we are, sixty-five years later and still together."

All of a sudden Abuelita would remember that she needed to add water to the beans. She would slowly get up and shuffle to the kitchen. No one wanted to move. No one wanted to break the spell.

Pepino was brown and white in color with a bright shiny nose. He came from a long line of Chihuahua dogs and he was so proud that he always pranced or strutted or jumped around.

CHAPTER XI
PEPINO Y BETO
(NO K STORY)

Pepino was José's pet dog. He was not very big but he could really yip-yap a lot. He had big ears that were always up and alert. His tail was always wagging and he was not afraid of anything. Pepino was brown and white in color with a bright shiny nose. He came from a long line of Chihuahua dogs and he was so proud that he always pranced or strutted or jumped around. He was just a bundle of energy.

Pepino loved to play with José. José would start by rubbing Pepino's head right between the ears. This told Pepino he was loved and this excited him even more. Pepino's favorite game was racing through the woods. José would run as fast as he could, dodging trees, jumping over small bushes, even splashing through the shallows in the *arroyo*. Pepino would not only run beside José, but with a burst of energy he could run rings around José and still stay up with him.

"Yap-yap, yap-yap," Pepino would call out as he ran around José.

All the noise would bring Beto the burro to the edge of his corral. Roberto was his name but José called him Beto. He was a little guy, so José called him Beto el Burrito. Beto had long floppy ears, strong sturdy legs and big eyes. Beto also had special coloring. He was brown and white except for a distinct cross formed by a long ebony line down his spine and another ebony line across his shoulders. Every *Domingo de Ramos*, Palm Sunday, Abuelito would tell the story of the reason burros bear the sign of the cross—Jesus entered the city of Jerusalem riding on a burro.

Beto loved to run. As soon as he heard Pepino and José racing, he too would start running along the fence. "Hee haw, hee haw!" Beto would call, as if to say, "Wait for me!"

José and Pepino used to come by the corral and whisper to Beto. Beto's ears would pop up as José rubbed his big head. Pepino would yap and jump as if to say, "Hey, Beto, it's your turn! Head rubbing feels good."

José was really happy to have two such good pet friends. He was very serious about their friendship. He made sure that they always had fresh water and were fed twice a day. Pepino would eat food scraps and José made sure that he did not get any greasy stuff because he understood that grease was not good for dogs. He also made sure there were no sharp bones so he would not get hurt eating. Beto ate mostly hay made from grass and sometimes alfalfa. Beto loved alfalfa for it was sweet and juicy. For a treat José would give Beto a carrot from the garden.

Together they were a happy trio. José, Pepino and Beto were together as much as they could be. They ran and jumped and made noise, but they also could sit very quietly in the shade of the big mesquite tree near Beto's corral. José would sit resting against the tree. Beto would put his big head through the fence and rest it on José's shoulder. Pepino would lie next to José with his feet up. He loved for José to rub his belly. José, Pepino and Beto would sit with each other in the cool shade and soon they would be asleep. What a great way to enjoy a *siesta* after a hard run!

CHAPTER XII
TÍO SIMÓN
(NO L STORY)

José enjoyed romping and resting with Pepino and Beto. As he rested under the shady mesquite tree, José thought of the many friends he had. He counted Nacho and Mando, his mom and dad, grandpa and grandma, his sister and oh yes, Tío Simón. Tío Simón was a grown-up but he was fun to be with because he seemed to know everything about everything. José suspected that what he didn't know he made up. At any rate he had something to say, no matter what subject José wanted to hear about.

One day José was confused about Tío Simón. So he asked him, "Tío Simón, are you my father's brother?"

"No," said Tío Simón.

"Then you must be my mother's brother," said José.

"Yes and no," said Tío Simón as a wide grin spread across his face.

José was now more confused but knew that Tío Simón was getting ready to start a story.

"I was born in Mexico just as your grandpa and grandma were," Tío Simón began. "I grew up near the big city of Querétaro in a tiny town with a funny name. Its name was *Rincón de Cama*—the Bed's Corner. In *Rincón de Cama* there were many chicken houses. That was the work everyone did. It was good work but the odor was not very nice. I was an orphan—my parents died when I was about ten.

"Then I stayed with my Tío and Tía but I had to work to earn my keep. They taught me everything about raising chickens. There were about five thousand chickens and some roosters in each house. My job was to feed them, make sure they had water and be certain that the big fans stayed on. Chickens do not sweat so they can die if they get overheated. I was taught how to spot the sick ones, and nurse and care for them. What I did not enjoy was working on the mountain of chicken droppings that the chickens produced. The odor was strong and it seemed to penetrate right through my skin. We had to remove the droppings every day because they attracted rats. Oh, how I hate rats!"

At this Tío Simón made a quick grab at José and José jumped, thinking it was a rat that was grabbing him.

Tío Simón continued, "After about two years I knew everything about chickens. Then I heard that the company that was part owner of the chicken houses was from the USA, and that it had even more and bigger chicken houses in a state named Texas. I heard too that they needed experienced chicken men in Texas. So I decided to go see if my fortune was waiting for me there.

"I was not a teenager yet but I started my journey anyway. I crossed most of Mexico on foot. I sometimes got a ride in wagons but most of the time I just put one foot in front of the other day after day. When I reached the *Río Bravo* I did not even stop. I just went right into it and swam across.

"Texas is harsh country but I was young and eager to find work. Soon I got to the northeast corner of Texas and there I found the chicken industry run by the same gringos that ran the chicken houses in *Rincón de Cama*. 'This is going to be easy.' I thought. 'The minute they see me, I can start my job for I know everything there is to know about chickens.'

"I soon found out that I was too young to get a job. The few words I knew that were not in Spanish were 'Yes sir' and 'Thank you very much'—and what's more, I had no documents. I had come so far with so many dreams, knowing no one, and here I was with no bed to rest in and no job.

"After begging for a few days, I decided to return to Mexico. In Mexico I had my Tío and Tía, and work in the chicken houses waiting for me. So I started my journey back.

"I had not gone far when I reached this *barrio*. It was dark and quiet. I thought I might find a soft bed of hay in the decaying barn where the burro was kept.

"As I sneaked into the barn, a noisy *perro*, a dog, started barking. Your grandpa came out to see what was bothering the *perro* and he saw me. I did not have time to run.

"When your grandpa saw me in the barn, he said, *'Qué estás haciendo, hijo?'*—*'What are you doing, son?'*

"*'Estoy cansado y tengo hambre, señor,'*—'I am tired and hungry, sir,' I said to him. Without hesitating, he asked me to come into the house. Your grandma fed me and fixed a bed for me to rest in. They had many kids but they made room for me. After many days of earning my keep by doing chores and tending to their chickens, I decided I did not want to return to Mexico. I wanted to stay here. I asked your grandpa for advice.

"'*Mi hijo,*' he said, 'You can stay with us. We can just add more water to the beans and make room for you.' And so I was adopted by your grandpa and grandma."

José did not know what to say. Tío Simón's story was more than he expected. He was very happy that Tío Simón had decided to stay and that Grandpa and Grandma had not hesitated to take him in, even though they had so many mouths to feed. Now he knew that Grandpa was not joking when he said, "The first ten kids are the hardest. After that they just take care of each other."

José shook his head as he thought of how his grandpa and grandma had twenty-four kids and room in their hearts to adopt one more.

For José, "school" signified access to books.

CHAPTER XIII
JOSÉ LEARNS ENGLISH
(NO M STORY)

The days in August felt as if they were getting hotter. The heat waves would rise in the distance. It looked as if everything was on fire. Abuelito Doroteo said that it was because it was "*la canicula.*" The word *canicula* sounded funny to José so he asked Abuelito to explain.

"Well," Abuelito said as he looked for a good place to sit on the porch, "in the old days a word for dog was 'can' and so when the August days turn very hot we say that not even the dogs are able to stand the heat."

When Abuelito said "dogs," José recalled that his teacher had talked about the "dog days of August" and how they were called that because the Dog Star was bright in a constellation in the sky. At any rate, the fact that he knew about the *canicula* did not cause the day to be cooler.

Soon, José knew, the school vacation would be over. In Texas the *canicula* not only signaled the end of the growing season for the tender vegetables but it also signaled the end of vacation. By the third week in August he would be back in school. No longer would he be able to play with his pets or go with his friends to the woods or the *arroyo*. Well, on weekends, he would squeeze in all the play he could.

José was excited because this year he would be in the third grade. He liked school but on occasion his head felt as if it was spinning. In school the teachers wanted everyone to learn English so they spoke only English to the students. His parents and grandparents spoke only Spanish. So José had to constantly switch English to Spanish and Spanish to

English. His brain was fast and he liked switching back and forth. On occasion he would answer in English when spoken to in Spanish or in Spanish when asked in English. He knew English but he was hesitant speaking it because he thought he had a thick accent. Switching back and forth was okay when he talked with friends, but when the teacher asked, he had to be sure to answer in English with his best pronunciation.

The teachers in his school were all nuns. Two were born in Guadalajara and knew Spanish very well. The other two were born in a place far away called County Cork in a country called Ireland. The first year of school, the children spoke only Spanish but by the end of the second year they started to learn English. The third year only English was spoken. The nuns were very patient with everyone. They just laughed as the children struggled with the languages on the playground. They would hear, *"Ven a jugar en los* swings," "Let's play on the swings," or when recess was over and the bell rang, the students would shout *"Ya sonó la* bell ring." It sounded funny but everyone knew what was being said.

José recalled his first English lessons. First he learned how to say "Thank you, Sister," and "Please, Sister." Once a day the second and third grade classes would sit together for their English lesson. Sister would open a huge book of slogans.

She would say, "You like it. It likes you. Seven Up."

Everyone would answer, "Jew lika eet. Eet lika jew. Seven oop."

"No, no," Sister would say. "It is not 'jew.' It is 'you.' It is not 'eet.' It is 'it.' It is not 'lika.' It is 'like.'"

And so they would repeat over and over again until they could clearly say, "You like it. It likes you. Seven Up." A few said it with a slight Irish accent but they all learned it.

Then Sister would go to the next slogan. This was great because it exercised the Spanish tongue that loved to trill "rrrrs," but had difficulty with the English words that had sounds like "th," "sh" and "ph." Sadly, though, there were few conversations where José could use his new-found slogan knowledge.

At any rate, hot or cold, *canicula* or not, soon it would be back to school for José. He liked school because he had a lot of questions about a lot of things. Papá, Abuelito and Tío answered countless questions, but he was learning that there were things in books that they did not know. Papá, Abuelito and Tío knew how to read but it was not what they really liked to do. They preferred telling stories through words or songs. José learned a lot with the stories they told and the songs they sang, but he was learning about the power of books. Once he learned to read, he found that he could go to any country or place in the world. He especially loved to draw pictures in his head as he lived through the adventures in the books. The big difficulty was that his parents owned no books in English and neither the *barrio* nor the little town had a library. For José, "school" signified access to books.

Yes, vacation was over and new worlds awaited José as he prepared to return to school. School would start soon enough. For now, José wanted to play with Pepino and Beto even though the days were hot, hot, hot!

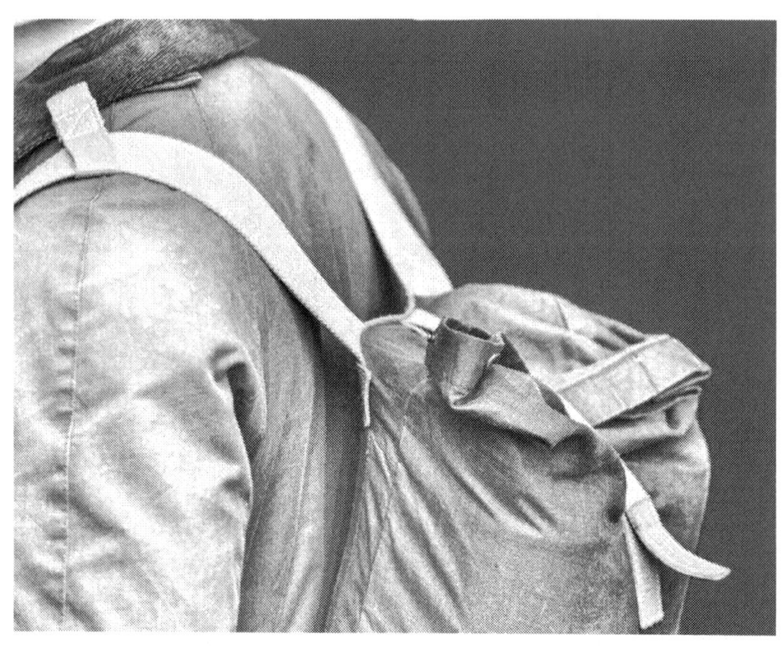

José's *mochila*, his backpack, was where he would carry all his school supplies with his food for the school day.

CHAPTER XIV
JOSÉ PREPARES FOR SCHOOL
(NO N STORY)

Way before the first day of school, José was excited. There was so much to do to get ready! He started to wear his shoes a week before school so his feet would get used to them (he had played barefoot all summer). He polished the shoes, made sure the laces were good. He especially made sure his toes fit right, for his feet got bigger as he grew. Luckily, the shoes still fit.

José made a list for Mamá of the items he remembered he used most last year. He wrote "Ruled white paper like the big kids use" at the top of the list. He added "ruler, eraser, colors." At the bottom of the list he added *"Dos plumas y tres lápices."* He wrote it this way so his *mamá* would be sure to see that he could write both ways.

Mamá was busy with José's clothes. The shirts he had would fit for a few weeks more. By that time she could sew two or three more shirts. She always bought cloth sacks of flour to save the beautiful material to make clothes. Some of the cloth had little ball players, others had squares, others were just light pastel colors. With the material she'd saved, she could sew at least three shirts for José. With the rest she would sew dresses for his sister. Mamá would also have to let out José's trousers for he grew a little taller that summer.

Mamá made a list too: "shirts, trousers, socks, jockey shorts, coat, gloves, cap." The "gloves, coat, cap" part of the list was just to be safe. Sometimes the early hours were cold but later it would warm up. She was glad their part of Texas was really ice-free all year. She was happy with the clothes she prepared. A tear came to her eye as she thought of how big her precious boy was. Her heart could see his beautiful smile as she wiped away the tear.

José's *mochila,* his backpack, was where he would carry all his school supplies with his food for the school day. Mamá would pack *tacos* wrapped with foil so they were still warm at mealtime. The surprise was to discover what type of *taco* Mamá had packed each day. Sometimes it would be *tacos de frijoles*, or *tacos de huevo, or tacos de huevo y chorizo*, sausage.

She always packed fruit as well as cookies which José ate with the cool juice she added. The juice *jarro*, jar, was just the right size to hold juice for two cookies. Sometimes she packed boiled eggs, which were José's least favorite food. They were good but they gave him gas. His classmates stayed away from him if he ate boiled eggs.

The school was close by. José had walked there for two years so he could hardly wait to see his other classmates who also walked to school. Together they would take care of each other—laugh, joke, eat their meals together shaded by the large mesquite tree.

José was excited that school would start the last week of August. As a third grader, he thought of himself as a big boy. This gave him a great idea. This year, he would ask his classmates to call him Pepe. José was for little boys. Pepe made him feel bigger. Already he felt taller —he strutted as he walked. Yes, he was Pepe. He would ask his *mamá, papá*, sister, everybody to call him Pepe because he was a big boy.

Summer was over. Pepe was eager for school to start. Pepe was ready.

CHAPTER XV
PEPE'S NEW BIKE
(NO O STORY)

Pepe. Yes, Pepe was his new name, and he reminded friends and family that he needed a new name because he was bigger. Because he was bigger, he must think bigger, eat bigger, help bigger, behave bigger. Just saying "BIGGER" made him feel bigger. Pepe was in the yard walking straighter and acting bigger when his father called him.

"Pepe, ven aquí," said his father.

Pepe quickly ran and sat by his father. *"¿Sí, papá?"* asked Pepe.

"J--, I mean Pepe, I have been thinking. My friend is selling his little truck. I have been riding my bike all these years. But I am thinking that a truck can be very useful carrying the fruits and vegetables. The bike and little trailer I use are small and the garden is getting bigger," said Pepe's father.

Pepe just listened. This was a big talk with his father.

Smiling, his father said, "But what will happen with my bike? Lacking use, it might rust."

"Papá," said Pepe, "put the bike in my care. I am big and can use a bike."

Pepe's father smiled. "Yes, I was thinking the same thing. Tell me, my big lad, when will the practice start?"

"When I get the bike," said Pepe, as he jumped up and started running.

The bike was in great shape. His father kept it clean, nicely painted and repaired. It had wide black tires with whitewalls and it was all red. The fenders were shiny because his father had just washed and waxed it. Even the chain guard was shiny. It had a large basket by the handlebars and a basket that straddled the rear fender. There were special screws where the little trailer was attached when Pepe's father carried the fruits and vegetables. The handlebars had been adjusted and the seat was just right. Pepe's legs reached the pedals just fine. What really pleased Pepe was that his father hadn't attached training wheels. He was big and he was sure he'd learn quickly.

His father said, "This bike has an especially wide seat and an especially wide kickstand. The seat helps make the ride easier and the kickstand keeps the bike steady as I display the fruits and vegetables."

Pepe wasn't listening, He was already picturing himself riding fast with the wind in his hair. But when he was in the seat and the kickstand was up, he had a different picture. He was unsteady and very shaky. Falling scared him.

His father smiled and said, "Relax. Just breathe deeply. Think hard and use the legs and arms. They will help balance the weight. It will take a little time but I will help."

Pepe watched as his father tied a big rake handle with string just under the seat. His father held the handle and ran behind Pepe as Pepe tried steadying the bike, steadying the handlebars, and pumping the pedals all at the same time. At first the bike went every which way. Pepe kept turning the handlebars right and left as he learned pedaling. This was much different than riding his friend's tricycle had been!

"Relax," cried his father as he ran behind Pepe. All the while, Pepe felt his father straightening the bike, making sure he didn't fall. Pepe felt like he was really speeding.

His father panted as he ran, all the while telling Pepe, "Steady, keep straight, keep the arms still, get a rhythm in the legs."

Pepe realized he was really having fun.

After circling the garden several times, Pepe wasn't afraid and wasn't even aware that his father wasn't running behind him. The rake handle was sticking up in the air like a flagstaff. His father was way, way back, breathing very hard, smiling as Pepe flew up the street.

Then Pepe started yelling, "I did it! I did it!" Pepe's father beamed with pride. Pepe was smart. He had learned fast.

After that first ride, Pepe started asking his *mamá,* "Is there anything we need at the market?" He asked Grandpa and Grandma if they needed anything. He asked all he met if they needed anything. He and his bike were at their service.

Pepe really liked riding his bike. He wiped it and cleaned it and made sure it was inside the barn when it rained. He liked riding fast with his little Chihuahua, all excited, running beside him. Pepe's hair was always messed up, bugs smacked him in the face and he jangled when the bike hit the ruts in the street, but he always had a big wide grin. Getting big sure was fun!

CHAPTER XVI
JOSÉ'S NAME
(NO P STORY)

José wanted everyone to call him by his big boy name and almost everybody did, for a while. Everybody, that is, but Abuelita. José's full name was José María Gonzales Rodríguez. A long name but one full of meaning and tradition. Abuelita had had many children. She had named two of them José but they had both died very young. It was customary to reuse the name of a sibling or close relative that had died, thus honoring the new life and memorializing the dead.

José's second name was uncomfortable for him. He never used it lest he be teased. María as a first name is always a girl's name. As a second name it is not uncommon for a boy. The tradition is that your second name is usually given to you when you are christened and it is usually the name of the saint's name on whose feast day you were born. José was born on December 8th which is the day Mary was Immaculately Conceived. So his second name was María. No one dared call him by that name unless they were looking for a fight. José María was fine but not just María.

José's third name was Gonzales. This was his father's last name. And so this was the name that he officially used when he registered for anything while in the United States.

Rodríguez was his fourth name. This was his mother's maiden name. Adding it to his name was very useful. For one, it honored his mother, and secondly, it meant that there would be less of a chance of being confused with anyone else. There might be another little boy named José María Gonzales but less of a chance of one named José María Gonzales Rodríguez. José once saw a book with all the names in town and their numbers and addresses. He found a bunch named John Smith and a handful named Billy Jones. He wondered if their mail was ever confused.

Abuelita was the only one that always called him José or Joselito. He did not mind for she had called him by this name since the day he was born. She called him by this name as a sign of her love, and because she remembered her two little babies in heaven.

CHAPTER XVII
MANOLO'S TRUCK
(NO Q STORY)

Manolo started by clearing land by the *arroyo*. The soil was rich and black and the *arroyo* flooded the area at least once a year after the two growing seasons when he could cultivate. The floods brought rocks onto the area but also more rich soil. Above the flood plain he planted peach, plum and pear trees. The pecan trees were in another area and they had been there for a long time. The pecan trees were producing but the fruit trees would not bear fruit for a few years.

At first the *huerta,* garden, was small and produced just enough to eat at home and to share with the neighbors. He expanded the *huerta* so he would have some produce to sell at the market. The *tomates* (tomatoes), *frijoles* (beans), *calabacitas* (zucchini), and onions grew in abundance. Manolo put them in a sack, threw it over his shoulder and walked to market where he set up a small *puesto* or stall. The next year he had a bumper crop, so he bought a *carretilla*, a wheelbarrow. This was great, especially for the root vegetables like *papas* (potatoes), carrots and beets. But when Manolo added corn, the *carretilla* was just not enough. This is when Beto the faithful burro was given an added job.

Manolo made two large baskets on a harness which Beto could carry with ease. Manolo expanded his stall at the market and Licha tended it for a few hours. This arrangement worked well until the people who operated the *mercado,* the city market, made a new regulation. They contended that live animals were unsanitary, they smelled and drew flies, and so they were banned from the *mercado.* Beto was out of a job.

Resourceful Manolo found two old bicycles. One he repaired to tip-top condition. The other he took apart. With one frame he fashioned a hitch so he could attach it to the bicycle and detach it again. With the remainder of the second bike and some old lumber, he built the semblance of a trailer and attached the two wheels. He now could carry his produce to market and comply with all rules.

Hard work and dedication paid off. The *huerta* grew and the fruit trees started producing. What's more, people asked Manolo to stop by their houses to deliver his produce so they would not have to go to the *mercado*. And that is when Manolo saw the need for a truck.

Paco, Manolo's friend, and his family were migrant workers. They would go north following the crops. They would go all the way to the state of Michigan to pick cherries, then turn around and do second pickings on crops like cotton on the way home. At this time most crops were harvested by hand and Paco's family, his wife and twelve children, were ready to work any crop, except maybe weeding beets. Bending over all day really hurt your back and the pay was not great.

One year Paco came home with a pickup truck. The family rode in the big covered flatbed truck and two of his sons drove the pickup. The truck was a nice early 50s Ford. The salt from the winter roads up north was starting to eat the fenders, the roof paint was fading and after 150,000 miles, the motor needed a little tender love and care.

But to Manolo's eyes the pickup was beautiful. Paco had bought it because his sons had plans of fixing it up and selling it. Manolo had no cash but he really wanted the truck. He struck a bargain. He would help the boys get the truck in fair shape and he would supply the family with produce. And he would hire the boys to tend his garden while he expanded his market hours and began his delivery service.

Little money exchanged hands but everyone gained. Paco had food for his family, the boys had jobs for the off-season, Manolo got a truck and help with his garden, but best of all, old Beto the burro could rest and José got his beautiful bike.

CHAPTER XVIII
LAND
(NO R STORY)

Manolo stood looking at his plot. He was pleased at what he saw, especially when he thought of what it looked like when he began.

Manolo and Licha wedded and decided to stay by his *papá y mamá*. Of the twenty-some siblings, fifteen made it to adulthood, and all but Manolo lived in distant towns. The jobs they had dictated the towns they lived in.

With the wedding money they got as gifts and the little they had saved, Manolo and Licha had enough to buy a small lot next to Papá *y* Mamá. They built a simple dwelling which they called the Love Nest. They had no city utilities then, but Manolo built an outhouse close by and they made do with a wood stove.

Manolo toiled as a day hand. He would go into town and wait at the plaza until someone would come by needing men. He would do almost anything. Sometimes feeding cattle, sometimes digging ditches all day. He saw no shame in toiling honestly to feed his family. Licha was a housemaid. She cleaned, cooked and did the washing.

Manolo's plan was to clean a space behind the house big enough to cultivate vegetables and legumes to supplement the staple of beans. He took out some spiny bushes and weeds and cleaned out a nice big space. That beginning season they ate the tomatoes, onions and *chili picante* he had planted, just to test the soil. The well he had dug supplied enough *agua* to use in the house and to keep the plants moist.

But Manolo had a vision. He wanted to cultivate enough land to yield vegetables to not only eat at his table but enough to sell in town. So he had his eye on the five lots adjacent to his lot that extended all the way down to the aquatic flow. Manolo and Licha toiled day and night, lived simply and saved as much money as they could. Still, it would take a long time to save enough even to make a down payment. So Manolo came up with a second plan.

All his siblings lived out of town and he had stepped up to tend to Papá *y* Mamá as they aged. If they could help just a little, Manolo would have enough to make the down payment. This way Manolo would have his *milpa* (field), he could give Papá something to do as his age and ailments affected his health, and he would tend to Papá *y* Mamá's daily needs. Although all the siblings liked the idea, some could not donate much. Manolo did not want to squeeze anyone, so he told them that even a little would help. And so Manolo had enough to at least begin the talks to get the land.

The man who owned the land saw Manolo as a godsend but somewhat as a fool. He lived two towns away. His mom had left the land to him in a will and he had no intention of coming back to town, no plans to use the land. Yes, he wanted to sell! The man could not believe that Manolo wanted to buy land on a flood plain, land full of stones, mesquite saplings and all kinds of spiny bushes.

Ah, but Manolo did not just see the land as it was, but as it could be—with the toil of his hands and his back—and he had no intention of letting his family down. He bought it at a giveaway amount. A vision without action is just a vision. So Manolo thanked God and began the long task of making the vision an actuality.

He walked the land deciding how much to begin to clean and the best beginning point. He fashioned a padded vest which he fitted on Beto. Long lines hung by Beto's sides. Beto would wait patiently while Manolo dug at the base of a bush with a *tlalache* (mattock), then tied the lines to the bush, and then Beto would pull. Out came the bush. Beto would then wait until the next bush had been loosened. By this method they cleaned the big space Manolo had designated as the beginning of his *milpa*.

The next step was not as easy. Manolo tied a big piece of canvas to Beto's lines. Beto would again wait patiently as Manolo put stones on the canvas, now a sled. Beto would tug and pull until he got to the place Manolo had deemed a good place to begin the wall. It was not exactly a high wall. It was just high enough to define the path a flood would take. It seemed like a million stones of all sizes, but at last they had moved all the ones it was easy to get to.

Manolo was pleased as he dug his hands in the beautiful loamy flood plain soil. In his mind he could see and smell the plants beginning to bloom.

Manolo was not finished with Beto. A well at the top of the *milpa* had to be dug as well as a wall and a little stone walkway so the well would not just be a mud hole. It took time, but the well got dug, and Manolo found an old hand pump at an antique shop. He fixed it and it was exactly what he needed.

Now he could begin the next phase: planting.

CHAPTER XIX
LA HUERTA
(NO S STORY)

Manolo had had the opportunity to live in Mexico for a while with a relative. Tío Plutarco lived near a town called León in the province of Guanajuato. Plutarco had a big family and a *milpa*, a large garden, for every one of the five adult children. He tended an even larger one for the remaining family. He knew how to manage a *milpa* and Manolo made certain he learned all he could.

Manolo looked at the *milpa* he had laid out on the flood plain and knew the time to begin had come. Now he could apply what he had learned in Mexico. A pecan tree grew at each corner of the garden, and above the flood zone he planted a peach tree, a plum tree and a pear tree. No, he did not really plant a tree. He planted a peach pit, a plum pit and a little pear *pepita*. Manolo had patience and looked to the future.

He knew that each plant had a different requirement. The plant that grew underground like the carrot did not mind another carrot nearby, but not very near. A tomato needed plenty of area to grow and breathe. An onion did not mind being near another plant except for the big white onion that wanted plenty of room. A vine plant like the *pepino* (cuke), the *melón* (cantaloupe), the *zucchini* and the *camote* (yam) required an even larger area.

Manolo planted the underground growing plant like the potato and carrot in a row. In addition, the onion, *lechuguilla* (lettuce), *betabel* (beet) and *rábano* (turnip) were each planted in a row. He made a little hill for each vine plant. On any given hill, he would plant corn at the very top, then *chili dulce* (bell pepper), *chili picante* (hot pepper) or *frijol* (pinto bean) on the incline.

With the method of placing the plant where it could develop unimpaired, Manolo maximized the utility of the land and the variety of the crop. Of equal importance for a good yield were the large channel and the little tributary web Manolo built from the well to the garden. A dream come true from the work of many, he called the garden on the flood plain EDEN.

Sunrise signals all coop dwellers and crowing, cackling, cheeping and clucking begins. Fowl seem happier when making noise.

CHAPTER XX
SOUND
(NO T STORY)

A cacophony of sound arises each sunrise and awakens all barrio dwellers. Every barrio being feels sharing sound is neccssary. Birds sing or chirp or peep. No one knows why. Maybe birds love sharing songs of love and praise, or maybe songs of warning and danger. Anyway, bird songs are heard by all as darkness is chased away by sunrise.

Guinea hens and peacocks are louder. Squawks and screeches are heard from afar. Crazy birds like guinea hens sound off for no good reason. Hens make noise all day. Sunrise signals all coop dwellers and crowing, cackling, cheeping and clucking begins. Fowl seem happier when making noise. Nannies baa-baa when hungry and hunger is unceasing.

Now, dogs also have a way of adding a unique sound. *El barrio* had small Chihuahua dogs who yap-yapped for any reason. Big hounds liked howling while mid-sized dogs and pups bark-barked, joining everyone else.

Pigs make happy squeals while rolling and sloshing in cool mud puddles. A key choice for pigs is cool over clean and an oink expresses joy of life. Burros make noise only when laughing. Hee-haw, hee-haw means life is good—come run and play! A neigh or whinny from a horse means hello, and running is his play and exercise. A cow, however, will only moo when hungry or when in need of relief. Milking is very necessary and no day may be missed.

Humans also shared in making daily noises in *el barrio.* Alarm clocks were superfluous when everyone was making a din. Radios playing *cumbias*, *corridos*, polkas and love songs, cars coughing, wheels screeching and horns honking added even more noise. Sounds like "*Huevos* are ready" or "*Adiós*, I love you" or "¡*Sí,* Mamá. I'm up!" were cries which added joy and music when *el barrio* began a new day.

Yes, *el barrio's* daily cacophony was music for happy or even weary souls. Everyone rejoiced in *barrio* life while dreaming of life elsewhere.

CHAPTER XXI
LA COCINA
(NO U STORY)

El barrio had a distinct odor. Some said it smelled. Others smiled and said, "*Cierto*, it has an aroma." Well, José liked being in his grandma's kitchen more than anywhere else in the *barrio*.

Everyone called her Mamá Antonia, and her *cocina* (kitchen) had great aromas that wafted to all the *barrio.* With so many children, she always had something cooking on her big wood stove. Sometimes the wood blaze alone filled the air with a warm relaxing scent.

Mamá Antonia started her day at five in the morning. The birds had started their morning praise, but the rooster had not yet started to crow. Her first task was to start a large pot of pinto beans. She had cleaned the beans the night before and let them soak all night. Before lighting the fire, she added a piece of salt pork and a piece of potato to the beans. The soaking and pork, she said, gave one less gas and the potato thickened the broth.

Next she made certain the *comal* (griddle) was hot. She started making the daily stack of *tortillas*, both corn and wheat. Stacks of three dozen *tortillas* of each kind were eaten by the end of the day. White bread was not for meals; it was eaten in a dessert called *capirotada*, a tasty concoction of sweetened bread, cheese, raisins, milk and a lot of cinnamon—and wow, was it good! She only made *capirotada* in Lent.

While rolling, flipping and stacking *tortillas* she stirred a large pot of *atole*, porridge. It might be of cream of wheat, rolled oats, rice or corn meal. This *atole* was the staple for breakfast every morning. Even when all the children were gone she still made a big pot of *atole* every morning. The neighbors loved it.

When the beans were done, they were refried in a big cast iron skillet and eggs were added. Now all was ready for breakfast—bean/egg *tacos* and *atole*. Sometimes instead of eggs, pan-fried potatoes were added.

Her *cocina* was the training place for all the girls of the barrio. Breakfast was simple. The rest of the meals were more elaborate and gave off even more great aromas. A meal was not a meal if it did not have Mexican rice, beans, *tortillas* and *salsa picante*, which was simply called chili. *Pollo* (chicken) or pork were sometimes added to the rice. Beef was eaten maybe once a week.

The delicacies were Mamá Antonia's specialty. She made cheese or meat *enchiladas* that left one licking all ten fingers and the plate. *Tacos* were part of the daily fare for school. Other great dishes that gave off great aromas were *carne asada*, and delectable *tamales*, which took an entire neighborhood to make, for they made fifty to ninety dozen at a time. *Caldos* (stews or broths) of all kinds and with a variety of vegetables were made. The family was so big that the *cocina* was constantly in action.

Mamá Antonia always wore an apron, a bandana and a big smile. No one visited and did not eat. There never were any leftovers. She had Joselito take the spare food to the old widows, sick neighbors or ladies who had recently given birth. Her words of wisdom were "If it is not moving, eat it. If it is moving, wait for it to stop, then eat it."

CHAPTER XXII
BAILE
(NO V STORY)

The sounds of music in a *barrio* are joyous and constant. Not only do they affect daily attitudes but also the hopes and dreams of people in the *barrio*. When you walk, you just don't walk. You prance or dance or practice your fancy steps. All in *el barrio* like music and many can play an instrument.

Of course all the residents of José's *barrio* thought they could sing and imagined how sexy or romantic they would look on stage. José decided he wanted to learn how to play the guitar, so Manolo put down his hoe and dusted off his old plunker. José showed some promise.

At first he liked the mournful yells the best, for he imagined himself a *mariachi*. The *mariachi* style of dress and rhythms were born in Guadalajara, Mexico's second largest city. When the French ruled the city, they had a great impact on the culture although they did not rule for long. For weddings the French wanted music but they had none to few French musicians, so they recruited local musicians with a limited assortment of instruments and dressed them in French period costumes with the lace, big shiny *conches*, tight pants, short jackets and a large colorful fluffy bow tie.

Of course the Mexican wanted to keep his sombrero so it was decorated and added to the ensemble. The French root word for wedding is "mariage" and so they were known as marriage players—hence, "mariachi." The rhythms were and are a blend of Spanish, French and indigenous styles.

José learned to play the guitar and how to yell with passion. As a teenager he heard music from different eras. *Barrio* men had gone to war and returned humming Big Band swing music as well as talking about the jitterbug and the lindy-six. From the south came the *cumbia* from Colombia and the *mambo* from Cuba. Local music was the most popular because area performers played it on the radio constantly. For full effect, most music was best played by a band. Area music sounded great when played by a trio. Essential for a trio was the accordion, accompanied by a guitar and a drum. If you added a sax, trumpet, bass or bass guitar, it then became a *conjunto*, a combo.

The accordion was an interesting choice. German immigrants introduced the instrument to Texas. They played the keyboard with the right hand and the left hand the button panel. Mexican musicians embraced the instrument, adapting it and played it predominantly with only the keyboard.

Accordion tunes, especially the polka, were also incorporated. The polka "Herr Schmidt" became "La Raspa," and the Mexican polka was born. The trio worked well for Tejano and Norteño music as well as traditional ballads, *corridos* and also waltzes. So José had many choices of music to learn to play. He found the trio the easiest ensemble to play in.

In that part of Texas the railroad had been the lifeblood of transportation. In the early days the train used steam engines. This meant they needed water. And so water towers were built about fifteen miles apart. Small communities grew around the tower. These agricultural towns needed a social outlet.

This outlet took the form of dances. On Saturday nights there usually was a dance where two or more nearby towns would participate. It would be at a city square, a dance hall or just in someone's swept backyard dirt patio. The most popular locale was known as a *plataforma.* A rancher would pour a huge concrete slab in his woods, in a wooded area so he could control the car parking. The *plataforma* had a small stage at one end for the musicians, and bolted-down benches all around the remaining sides. Opposite the stage was the gate, a break in the benches. Men bought a ticket which they pinned to their shirt. Women and children did not need tickets.

Around the *plataforma*, about ten feet from the edge, the rancher would build a series of stalls or booths which he rented out. You could buy *tacos* at one or a whole meal of *arroz con pollo* (chicken and rice), or *enchiladas con frijoles*, potato salad, and flour or corn *tortillas*. Other booths sold drinks, mainly *aguas*—water with lemon, orange, watermelon and other fruits. Best José liked the *agua de orchata*—rice water with cinnamon. There was also a booth where you could buy, of all things, hamburgers. They also sold Cokes which were most popular with teenagers. A teen's best choice was a *raspa* or snowcone with a scoop of ice cream in it.

The games of chance including bingo always attracted a crowd. The booths had all sorts of food, sweets and drinks, except for beer. Beer was sold at a special booth further into the woods and away from the family area.

José started playing in a trio. He really liked being on stage playing and smiling at the girls. Unfortunately José also liked to dance. Soon he stopped playing and started dancing. He would be dancing along and beside him would be Manolo and Licha or his *abuelita* and *abuelito*. Sometimes it would be the girl's parents and he had to make sure he was not holding her too closely.

When the trio played "In the Mood" or "Stardust," the floor filled up quickly with the old folks. Few musicians knew how to read music, but Glenn Miller would surely be impressed with those tunes played with so much passion on an accordion, guitar and drums.

The young people danced the *cumbias* with wild abandon, and all did the polka laughing and competing with fancy steps. No, not the straight-legged skip-hop-run German polka, but the hold-them-close, swish-your-bottom, and glide with a swoosh-swoosh Mexican polka. To help the slide and glide, corn meal was strewn on the concrete. The swoosh-swoosh could be heard from far away as well as the laughter.

The best dances were during the special feast days, and they were many of them! There was *Cinco de Mayo*, when a great battle was won against the French; *el Día de la Independencia*, commemorating Mexico's independence from Spain; *el Día de los Muertos*, the Day of the Dead; the feast of *Nuestra Señora de Guadalupe*, on the 12th of December; and of course Easter, Christmas and New Year's. On these days the church would sponsor a big *jamaica*—a huge fiesta with plenty of food and a dance. All were ready to dance anytime and anyplace.

The ultimate dance was *Día de la Independencia*, on the 16th of September. Before the dance there would be a big parade with floats and bands and marchers from different organizations. Other towns would send floats or marching groups. Queens and their escorts were chosen by popular election, and sometimes dignitaries from Mexico would attend. José could hardly wait for the speeches and formalities to end so the dance would start, for on these special dances a big band would play.

Yes, life was good when there was a *baile* to look forward to!

[La curandera] provided not only some medical relief but psychological and emotional relief as well. She kept our cultural and ethnic beliefs alive.

CHAPTER XXIII
LA CURANDERA
(NO W STORY)

Every *barrio* must have a *curandera* or healer. A *curandera* is essential because she is the first responder for any medical emergency, including delivering a baby. Yes, it is usually an experienced female and she is on call 24/7. If you go to a doctor you can count on the first question being "Have you seen the *curandera* yet?" You see, the rule is to call the *curandera* first. If she is unable to handle the situation, call the priest—then you can go to the doctor.

Doña Juana is the *curandera* in Jose's *barrio*. She has delivered almost all the *barrio* babies. She is prepared for any emergency. Her bag is huge, for it is full of bandages for sprains, broken bones, sores, or to hold the mustard packs, herb patches or even the most important medication, a Vicks VapoRub chest liniment. She carries herbs teas, ointments, mercurochrome, a red tincture she called *Sangre de Chango*, monkey blood. Just in case, she carries a large rubber bottle and tubing for enemas. Her grandson and his bike stand by outside in case the priest or doctor are needed.

In her house Doña Juana dries herbs on the sparkling clean stucco of her front room. From these herbs she makes teas, each having a special medicinal use. She has *manzanilla* (chamomile) tea for upset stomachs, cinnamon tea, lemon grass tea and other exotic teas like *Oreja de Ratón*, mouse ear tea. She makes that special tea from a plant she finds in the shade of mesquite trees. Its leaves are in the shape of a mouse ear.

Babies and children keep her very busy. Young mothers reeling from lack of sleep, their crying babies in distress, come to her. No problem! Doña Juana gets right into action. She diagnoses it as *empacho*, colic. She certainly has seen this before. Tepid olive oil is rubbed all over the baby's body, especially on the tummy. The baby is then put on its tummy and she massages the small of his back using plenty of oil. A cloth is placed over the baby's back, and Doña Juana pinches a fold of skin through the cloth. She pulls gently but firmly until she hears a "pop". This means the adjustment is complete. Doña Juana sends them home carrying a pouch of special tea to calm and soothe the mother and also the baby as it digests its mother's milk.

The second most common baby ailment she treats is one common in Mexican culture. If one sees a baby, admires the baby's ruddy cheeks, chubby legs or cute smile but does not touch the baby, it develops a fever. The baby has been exposed to *Mal Ojo*, the Evil Eye. The best cure is for the parents to find the thoughtless person and have them caress the baby.

If the person is not found, though, Doña Juana is called to do her magic. She starts by rubbing slightly heated olive oil all over to cleanse the body. She then takes an unbroken, uncooked egg and rubs it all over the baby's body. This is to give the fever's heat a path for leaving the body. All the time she is praying. The egg is broken and placed in a small dish. A cross made from dried blessed palm from the last Palm Sunday Mass is placed on the yolk. The albumen part of the egg has already started to cook from the transferred body heat. By morning the fever breaks and the baby returns to normal. *El Mal Ojo* is no match for Doña Juana.

The oddest ailment Doña Juana treats is El Susto. In this ailment the patient, young or old, is frightened by something heard, seen, or experienced—frightened so much that the spirit leaves the body. The patient becomes lethargic and feverish.

The ritual requires a larger arsenal for Doña Juana. She gathers the ever-present blessed olive oil, an unbroken egg, lime from the tool shed, ruda (rue, an aromatic plant), and the dish and palm. She also needs a handkerchief and *agua bendita* from the church's fountain. A candle and a crucifix are set on a little table in the room. The patient is placed on his or her back. Doña Juana starts praying and passing the rue over the entire body. A cross is made of the rue and placed under the sheets. A paste is then made by mixing the olive oil and lime. Using the paste, a cross is made on the forehead, the chest and on the inside of the joints of the arms and legs. The trusty egg is then rubbed all over the body, to remove the fever's heat, and then cracked into the dish. A palm cross is placed on the yolk of the egg and the dish placed under the bed to be examined the next morning.

Curious José, hidden behind Doña Juana, liked to see the next part of the ritual. She covered the patient's face using the clean handkerchief. She then took a big mouthful of the *agua bendita*, pursed her lips and forcefully sprayed the handkerchief-covered face. She did this three times. She then lifted a corner of the handkerchief, leaned over and softly said *"Espírito de* [patient's name], *vente. No me dejes."* This means "Spirit of [name] come. Don't leave me." A full five decades of the rosary later, the ritual ended. The patient fell soundly asleep, and an exhausted Doña Juana headed home.

On call at all times, she performed these and many more services out of a sense of duty and love. Her compensation sometimes consisted of a couple of dollars, but more often a good meal or a bag of baked goods. She provided not only some medical relief but psychological and emotional relief as well. She kept our cultural and ethnic beliefs alive. For her contributions she gained the respect of all and kept food on her table.

Abuelita never forgot to send her a small pot of her *atole.*

CHAPTER XXIV
SPOOKY
(NO X STORY)

There was no lack of imagination in the *barrio*. Someone was always telling a story they heard or lived through or were just inventing. The stories served a purpose. They distracted the listener from the hardships of work or daily living; they entertained; they educated; they reminisced; or they warned folks back to the straight and narrow path. The best stories were those told by the old folks about the old country. The children would be mesmerized and the adults smiled as they recalled when they first heard the story, and knew that one day it would be their children's turn to tell the story, adding their own flair. Thus the essence of the stories would live from age to age, from generation to generation.

A favorite pastime was to get Abuelito or Abuelita to sit by an open fire in the patio or even around the table and continue the game of *"el cuento de nunca acabar,"* the story without end. No one really knew when but a long time ago, maybe when Mamá and Papá were young, a character had been chosen and, each time they gathered, a new adventure or situation would be imagined, and so the story never ended as long as the imagination kept it alive. José could not wait for his turn to introduce a new twist to the saga or a new character to accompany the old one. And so it went on and on, and may still be going on today in the hearts and memories of many.

The first story José could remember was El Cucui, the bogeyman. He knew to not mess with or doubt El Cucui. El Cucui is a story that originated in Spain, then incorporated and amplified with ancient indigenous legends learned in the New World. Some say El Cucui is the opposite of a guardian angel. Others say it is a shapeshifter, sometimes a big black bird, sometimes a shadow, sometimes on a rooftop, sometimes under the bed or in a closet. To José it did not matter what it looked like. He knew it was always watching and it was what it did that terrified him.

The story was usually told when little ones were misbehaving and would not settle down and go to sleep. The story in song said, “Go to sleep, little one, or El Cucui will come get you, take you to his cave and eat you.” The wind blowing and the night noises verified that El Cucui was near. To avoid becoming a Cucui *taco,* the best thing to do was to quiet down and go to sleep. Sometimes an overactive imagination and El Cucui could invoke a visit by Doña Juana for a *Curada de Susto!*

If you outgrew El Cucui, you weren’t home free. Another shapeshifter was literally “in the wings.” For boys, young men or even irresponsible older men, La Lechuza was watching them. A *lechuza* is a barn owl, but don’t let that fool you. It is said that there once was a woman who by day was a beautiful lady, but by night she turned into a hag and a witch. As the story goes, a man felt rejected by the beautiful lady, spied on her and revealed her secret. The men came to deal with her and she shapeshifted into a barn owl, a *lechuza.* Now in revenge, she watches men who are out at night misbehaving, being where they should not be, doing what they should not do. When she spots a candidate, she morphs into a gigantic black bird-woman. Her wingspan is huge and makes a rushing sound. She has the face of an old hag and her screeches curdle your blood and make you wet your pants. She has big claws to grasp at you and an eerie red light shines from her stomach to spot you.

Once in the spotlight, the instinct is to run for home, running in the dark through mud, brambles, over wooden or barbed wire fences. When you stumble into the house disheveled, all scratched up, bug-eyed and out of breath, you don't have to say a word. Everyone will know you have seen La Lechuza. What's more, they will know you were not behaving. And just to make sure you stay home and do not forget she was watching, from now on you can hear her in the night. Sometimes she sounds like a baby crying, taunting you, or screeching, howling like the wind, or even like birds chirping when they should be asleep. La Lechuza has deterred frequent outings and sometimes prompted a visit by Doña Juana and her assortment of herbs and rituals.

The quintessential legend in the Spanish language is La Llorona, the Wailing Woman. This story was usually told by Abuelito who swore he had seen her or at least heard her. It was told to keep young children at home and away from any body of water, especially at night. According to Abuelito, back in his village or in a village nearby in Méjico, he knew a man who had also seen her and another man said he knew someone whose children were taken one night, never to be seen again. Abuelito always started the story in almost a jovial voice, then got serious and when he went into his scary voice, the wide-eyed children jumped and looked around to make sure nothing was sneaking up on them.

Abuelito would start with, "There was a beautiful Indian girl named María. She was the prettiest girl in the village. She had long shiny black hair, large dark sparkling eyes, cinnamon-colored skin and a smile that made young men swoon. One day a very handsome young man, elegantly dressed, riding a huge white horse, rode into the village. He was an *hidalgo*—the son of somebody important. When he saw María walk by, he instantly fell in love with her. As time went by, he built a small house by a nearby cool running river. By and by their love produced two children.

"Frequently he would ride off for weeks at a time as he inspected the family's vast lands. She always waited in anticipation for him, for she loved him very much. One day she saw a great ornate carriage drawn by prancing white horses. Her heart jumped with joy. María knew that he was coming to take her and the children away to one of his haciendas and a better life. When the carriage stopped he jumped off, but instead of running towards her, with great flair he opened the door to the carriage and assisted a young woman who was all dressed in a flowing white gown.

"María's heart sank as she heard him say 'María, may I present to you my wife.'

"María, stuttering, said 'But I am your wife! These are your children!'

"He replied, 'I never married you. I married this lady. She is of my own class and yes, these are my children. That is why I am taking them with me. They will be raised in my culture. Get them ready. Tomorrow my men will come to get them and their things.'

"María collapsed while holding her two babies.

"Early the following morning, she heard the sound of horses. The men were coming for her babies! María took the children in her arms, ran out the back door and hid amongst the reeds in the river. She watched and heard as the men ransacked her home. As the men came out the back door she panicked, grabbed the children and submerged them and herself in the murky water. She soon came up gasping for air. The men were gone but so were the babies. In desperation she searched the river and the river bank. Not finding her babies, she lost her mind and drowned.

"It is said," Abuelito would add in a whispery voice, "María will not be allowed into Heaven, until she found the souls of her babies. She now roams all bodies of water wailing *'Dónde están mis hijos?* Where are my babies?' María is now an old ugly woman dressed in white as she searches the banks of rivers, arroyos, ponds and lakes. She cannot find her own babies so she will take any child who is out at night by the water's edge."

By this time José and the other children listening would be scooched up to their parents. On nights when the wind howled, they were sure La Llorona was looking for anyone outside.

This story was not only meant to keep the young ones close to home. It was also an object lesson for young ladies to choose wisely when they marry.

Storytime was an essential time in the *barrio*. It was not just a social pastime but a way to stress morals, responsibilities and a sense of belonging to a family, a wider community and revered ancestors.

José learned his religion more through example and deed than from the words preached or read.

CHAPTER XXV
CHURCH
(NO Y STORY)

Nuestra Señora de Guadalupe is the heart of the Mexican Catholic faith. Some think Mexicans, because of their devotion to her, are *Guadalupanos* and not Catholics. So, *Nuestra Señora de Guadalupe* was the name of the parish where José's *barrio* worshiped. The town's Mexican-American Catholics pooled their resources and talents and constructed a parish complex, taking advantage of available old Air Force barracks to build a church, a four-room school (1st to 8th grades), a large hall for festivities and a small convent house for the nuns who came from Mexico and Ireland. The complex was located so as to service the four *barrios* in town. It was on the north side of the railroad tracks. The south side was where most of the Anglo homes were. Convenient to most, it was over a mile from José's *barrio.*

At first José's extended *familia* and friends in the *barrio* would walk the long mile in all kinds of weather to attend Mass. All intended to go. However, the women were more dedicated than the men. Some men had the attitude that said, "The wife is so devoted that she is going to Heaven for sure. All I have to do is hold on to her apron strings."

In José's *familia,* however, all went to church and all participated. José became an altar server as soon as he was old enough. He later joined the choir. He was a little sad because he was not allowed to use his skill with mariachi hollers, but he did like to sing.

As she grew older, José's beautiful sister Consuelo was often chosen Miss Queen for all sorts of occasions, from crowning the Blessed Mother to representing one organization or another in a parade.

Mamá and Abuelita belonged to the Altar Group and the *Guadalupanas.* The Altar Group made sure the altar was clean and adorned with fresh flowers before all services; the ladies also led the congregation in praise with the beads before each Mass. The *Guadalupanas* were the social services for the barrio. Bringing food to those in need, visiting the sick, helping new mothers and attending all funerals to sing and praise with those who had lost a loved one—all this was done with great seriousness and dedication.

As an altar server, José attended almost all the funerals. One widow was visited four times for her husband had died and three sons were killed in the war. She said she hated cars because each time one came to her house, it meant bad news. These two ladies' groups were also responsible for the week-long task of making several hundred dozen *tamales* for the annual church bazaar.

Papá and Abuelito were ushers and collected the donations at Mass. Papá also became crowd controller and peacekeeper when the church was full and the crowd overflowed outside, such as when ashes were distributed at the beginning of Lent, or when biannual Catholics came at Easter and Christmas.

The one organization Papá and Abuelito belonged to that José liked a lot was the Nocturnal Adoration group. The Blessed Sacrament was exposed on the altar and someone had to be present at all times for 24 hours. The men would choose which hour to be present. Papá never picked the easiest hour. He and Abuelito went from 2am to 3am. When José was asked to join them, his chest puffed up for this meant he was being accepted as an adult. This was like a rite of passage.

He soon learned another reason for his presence at the adoration hour. After working since the previous morning, the adults were tired. After a little while Papá and Abuelito would start nodding off. This was José's cue to start singing. Singing kept them awake at least for a little while so the three could finish praising with the beads.

José learned his religion more through example and deed than from the words preached or read.

CHAPTER XXVI
LESSONS LEARNED
(NO Z STORY)

El barrio was the crucible for José's formative years. There he was both shielded and exposed. He was shielded from the violence exacted on minorities outside the *barrio* as well as the discrimination experienced by adults. He was exposed to much positive reinforcement on values, potential and responsibility. He had role models, but many were in the "what not to do" category. The first generation, his parents, had the challenge of establishing the basics—i.e., language, shelter, food, jobs. They placed their hopes on the next generation. "*Uno de estos días,*" one of these days, was the dominant thought.

Everyone accepted the fact that education was the key to success. Education, however, was a great challenge, for access was limited, in some cases denied, and, although desired, not necessarily encouraged. The first generation was apprehensive. They themselves were learning the language. They had very little knowledge or access to the system and, on a more personal level, they were unable to help with homework past the 3rd or 4th grade. Like most parents they did the best they could with the capabilities and resources they had.

José's family saw potential in him. His quick mind, great curiosity and eagerness to learn inspired the family to encourage him. Mamá Licha taught him the importance of prayer, dreaming and empathy for others. José called her his avocado because, like the fruit, her heart was too big for her body. Like most mothers, Licha frequently said, "You can be whatever you want to be." She also stressed that focus and education were the way to make dreams come true. To José's delight, she also taught him to dance—and oh! Did she have rhythm!

Papá Manolo was a great moral role model. The barrio's bane was alcohol and in a very large family there were no gatherings without it. In the family multitude, he was the only one that did not drink any alcohol. He also did not smoke or drink coffee. His admonition was "Don't put anything in your body that you know is not good for you." José noted this and applied these lessons to his life as well.

Manolo did have a great sense of humor and this helped José to deal with social situations like discrimination. Just as importantly, José learned honesty, a great work ethic, loyalty to family and respect for everyone. He learned all this from example and it helped shape his life.

Abuelito taught young José the great importance of remembering his ancestors and the challenges they overcame so that he could be where he was today. He kept repeating the story about a burro to stress the point. "I once had a burro, a very smart burro. One day he decided to go out into the world. He was gone for a long time, saw a lot and learned even more. But when he came home, he was still a burro. A very smart burro, but a burro." José learned that he was not to forget where he came from and not to get too big for his britches.

Abuelito always stressed responsibility, particularly when it came to work. Even when working in the cotton field, he would stop and tell José, "See that man? He is paying you. When you don't do your job well, you are stealing from him and bringing shame on yourself." José listened and learned.

Abuelita taught José unselfishness and demonstrated unconditional love. She had many grandchildren and great-grandchildren and as she grew older she forgot names, but that did not slow her love down. Whoever was in front of her, that was whom she loved at that moment.

She prayed as she worked for she was concerned about everyone in the family and in the *barrio*. She would feed everyone in the family and *barrio* with her *atole*. Abuelita taught José how to slow-dance and this greatly delighted him. An important lesson he learned from her was "Don't go to heaven alone." José took this lesson to heart for the rest of his life.

In time José left the barrio armed with many lessons, knowing that he would be the vanguard for his generation in the family. He later learned a motto that put his mission into perspective: "Don't let the past dictate your future. Let the past enrich your future."

PHOTO CREDITS

Some of the photographs used in this book were provided by the author and his family. In most cases, however, the photographs used are copyright-free images from the web. Unsplash.com, Pexels.com, and Pixabay.com, among other sites, allow designers to access photographs without paying a royalty or fee. It seemed only fair, however, to credit the creators of these wonderful photos for their work, or identify our models if they are known. Here are the sources of all our photographs.

Cover Photo: Composite: Nathan Dumlao, Unsplash.com, and Aaron Burden, Unsplash.com

Page 8 Luke, Anthony and David Barrientes, 2021

Page 12 Michael Vines, Pixabay.com

Page 16 Greg Pedroza, 1947

Page 17 Luke Barrientes, 2021

Page 19 Thomas Park, Unsplash.com

Page 21 Composite: Ryan Riggins, Unsplash.com; Gretta Blankenship, Pixabay.com

Page 22 Anemone123, Pixabay.com

Page 25 Luke and Anthony Barrientes, 2021

Page 27 Anthony and Luke Barrientes, 2021

Page 29 Nathan Anderson, Unsplash.com

Page 32 Travis Grossen, Unsplash.com

Page 34 Karolina Grabowska, Pexels.com

Page 35 Filipe Leme, Pexels.com

Page 38 Rebeca Cruz Galvan, Pixabay.com

Page 47 Public Domain Pictures, Pixabay.com

Page 48 Martin Winkler, Pixabay.com

Page 52 Composite: Ryan Riggins, Unsplash.com; Rosa Menkman, personal permission

Page 54 Long Bún, Unsplash.com
Page 59 Jesse Schoff, Unsplash.com
Page 60 Jukka Heinovirta, Unsplash.com
Page 62 Composite: Qiangxuer, Pixabay.com; Chris Lee, Pixabay.com
Page 66 Darren Shen, Unsplash.com
Page 70 Bảo Minh, Pexels.com
Page 73 Mr. Xerty, Unsplash.com
Page 76 Rebeca Cruz Galvan, Pixabay.com
Page 78 Manny Becerro, Unsplash.com
Page 81 Autumn Barnes, Pixabay.com
Page 82 Gabriel Jimenez, Unsplash.com
Page 83 Composite: K. Mitch Hodge, Unsplash.com; David Mark, Pixabay.com
Page 84 Lewis Wilson, Unsplash.com
Page 85 Cristina Anne Costello, Unsplash.com
Page 86 Alex Dugan, Unsplash.com
Page 87 "Lola," courtesy of Reggie Barrientes
Page 88 Alessandro Cerino, Unsplash.com
Page 94 John Moeses Bauanm Unsplash.com
Page 96 Karen Bernardo
Page 98 Ava Sol, Unsplash.com
Page 106 Composite: Marek Studzinski, Unsplash.com; Diego Passadori, Unsplash.com
Page 108 Karisa Barrientes, 2021
Page 109 David Bernardo. This crucifix was made by the author.
Page 111 Greg Pedroza 1959
Page 114 David, Anthony, and Luke Barrientes, 2021

ABOUT THE AUTHOR

Gregorio C. Pedroza, Ph.D., and Elidia "Lilly" Elizondo have been married for 58 years. He served as a Captain in the U.S. Army, and was assigned to the Office of the Army Chief of Staff in the Pentagon during the Vietnam War. Gregorio retired from IBM as a senior engineer-project manager. He and Lilly live in Upstate New York. They have three children: a degreed registered nurse, a computer engineer employed by IBM, and a physician who graduated from the Harvard Medical School. The family is further enriched by ten grandchildren and five great-grandchildren.

Made in the USA
Columbia, SC
15 May 2021

37350157R00065